A Gift

Johnny Know-It-All

by Mary Woodbury

illustrated by Barbara Hartmann

A Hodgepog Book

All the characters in this story are ficticious.

Thanks to the Canada Council Block Grant programme and Alberta Foundation for the Arts. Thanks to Screaming Colour Inc. (a division of Quality Color Press Inc.), and Daana Downey and Kim Smith at Priority Printing. Thanks to Norman Amor—you know why.

Editors for the press: Luanne Armstrong, Peggie Graham & Candas Jane Dorsey. Cover and inside illustration copyright ©1996 by Barbara Hartmann. Cover design by Gerry Dotto. Inside design and page set-up by Ike at the Wooden Door, in Palatino (True-Type Font) in Word for Windows 6. Printed at Priority Printing, Edmonton, on 50lb. Offset White with Cornwall Cover.

A Hodgepog Book for kids.

Published in Canada by River Books, a member of the Books Collective, 214-21, 10405 Jasper Avenue, Edmonton, Alberta, Canada T5J 3S2. Telephone (403) 448 0590.

Canadian Cataloguing in Publication Data

Woodbury, Mary, 1935-
A gift for Johnny Know-it-all

ISBN 1-895836-27-1

I. Hartmann, Barbara, 1950- II. Title.
PS8595.O644G53 1996   jC813'.54   C96-910647-5
PZ7.W86Gi 1996

A Gift for Johnny Know-It-All

Mary Woodbury

Barbara Hartmann

DEDICATION

Dedicated to all the Grade Four children I have taught, either back when I was a young teacher or more recently as a visiting author or writer-in-residence in Edmonton Public Schools and across the province of Alberta.

ACKNOWLEDGMENTS

The author would like to thank her editors, especially Luanne Armstrong; Dr. Janet Marche for checking the medical details, and Sonny Marche for checking Royal Military College details and providing photographs for the artist Barbara Hartmann.

Chapter One

It started the day Miss Moore moved Bennie Snell to the seat behind me. The kid stinks. I mean he really stinks. Like he'd slept between a diaper pail and a pile of dirty socks. I thought I was going to bring up my Cheerios, all over the back of Angela Dunn's pink track suit.

My reaction was pretty fast.

"Miss Moore, maybe I should move closer to the front."

"Why's that, Johnny?" The teacher studied my face like it was a map of Canada. She's tall, not much older than my stepsister, with dark curly short hair that hangs over her eyes and thin arms that seem to be in constant motion. She's sporting a big diamond on her left hand so I know she has a boyfriend. She isn't wearing makeup or nail polish. Her black shoes need polishing. I don't think she's been teaching very long 'cause sometimes she looks like a lost kid. I help her as much as I can.

David Lee whispered from across the aisle. "Come on, Mr. Know-It-All, I dare you to tell her the truth." He squeezed his nose tight and waved his head in Bennie's direction.

"My eyes are sore." The inside of my mouth was dry. I

wanted a drink of water. The kids giggled.

Bennie had been at the back of the class, separated from the rest of us ever since the really bad weather had started. He'd punched David Lee in the stomach for saying he was dumb. He's been sitting between the reading corner and the table with the gerbil and the fish tank on it.

Miss Moore tilted her head to one side and stared at me, the way she does when she is deciding whether we are fibbing or not. She walked down the aisle and stood beside my desk, turned and looked at the board. "Everything looks pretty clear to me."

I tried to figure out some other reason for moving while I had her attention but the bell rang for recess. The girls filed out to get on their jackets and boots. Miss Moore checked her day book, picked up the chalk eraser and set to work, humming as she put the next lesson on the board. She works really hard.

I stuffed my math book into my desk, grabbed my granola bar and headed for the door. David Lee, skinny as a toothpick, wearing his dumb old Blue Jays cap backward on his pitch black hair, caught up with me and we crowded through the door.

"Boys," Miss Moore cautioned. I shrugged.

"What are we going to do?" David asked as we pulled on our jackets.

"Hey, Johnny, can you really fit those ears under your hat?" Tyler snickered. He's the tallest kid in our grade, and the one you don't want to tangle with, especially when you are the shrimp of the class like I am. I only weigh sixty pounds in my basketball high tops. I don't mind being short. My dad says plenty of famous people were short.

It's my ears I hate. I really hate my ears. They stick out from my head like handlebars on a bicycle. I sleep on the right one, one night, and the left one the next, hoping to flatten them.

Over by the fence a gang of Grade Four boys was building a snow slide. What a motley crew we are! That's what my dad would say. Rich, poor, fat, skinny, smart and slow, noisy, shy, you name it, that's our class. David and I joined them. That's when I noticed Bennie Snell following us. Noticed is not the word, smelled is more like it. I smelled him coming. He was humming, humming the tunes we were going to sing at the school concert the day before school ended for the Christmas holidays. I was the star performer.

See, I've got a gift, as my dad calls it. I can sing. I sing in the boy's choir at the cathedral and I sing solos in the Turner school choir, the one our teacher Miss Moore leads. When I sing I forget everything and disappear into the music. I even forget my ears.

Somehow having Bennie Snell coming up behind me like that really bugged me—his coat smelling like dead mice, his pale flat face with wide apart grey eyes looking permanently sad, his hands in mismatched gloves. There he was, coming behind us, sitting behind me in class, moving into my territory, humming my songs. I couldn't take it. I turned and yelled.

"Go away, Bennie. You stink."

Beside me David Lee gasped. The kids who heard me stopped trodding down the snow and stared.

"What did you say?" Bennie's head lifted. He'd been trudging along with his hands in his pockets.

I wanted to grab my words back like you grab snowflakes and toss them on your tongue. Snowflakes tingle. It wasn't my tongue that was tingling, it was the back of my neck. Bennie's face had turned red. He'd heard what I said all right. I gulped, and shouted.

"You stink like garbage. You stink like manure. You stink like wet skunks. You stink like..."

"Shut up, Johnny, he'll murder you." David tugged my arm, tugged me toward the teacher on yard duty. The old guy hadn't looked up yet.

I was so busy hurling insults at the kid I didn't see Bennie's right hand make a fist in the green ski glove with the hole at the knuckles. I was so busy filling the air with my voice like I do, shouting, using words like weapons. I've got a great vocabulary for my age. My dad says I should put a bodyguard on my tongue because I don't know when to shut up.

David told me after that he could hear the crunch of my glasses and my nose as Bennie's fist connected with my face. One blow and I was flat on my back, staring up at the dull grey sky, my head throbbing, major pain in my nose and the taste of blood in my mouth.

Next thing I knew Bennie and I were in the principal's office. I sat there holding a towel and a pack of frozen peas on my face and Bennie was slouched in the other chair rubbing his sore fist against his jean pant leg. My dad had been called from the bank. He leaned against the wall. Bennie's mom couldn't make it because she had her toddler napping, the school secretary said after she got off the other phone. Miss Moore stood in the doorway looking worried, angry and perplexed.

Mr. Anderson, the principal, towered over us. His face and ears were red. "You boys know the rules. At Turner School we debate, discuss and decide—we don't fight, tease or bully. You boys have disobeyed all the rules. What are we going to do with you?"

"He called me names," Bennie muttered.

"He hit me," I mumbled into the cold drippy mess around my nose and mouth. It hurt buckets. "I'll probably need stitches."

"There are no excuses. I'm disappointed in you. You are both suspended for a day. Miss Moore, when they come back I want these two boys assigned to work detail until the holidays, in the library and the computer room. One of you has a quick temper and the other a runaway tongue. I insist that you work that out. At Turner we are good neighbours and good students, most of all. Do you hear me? Johnny? Bennie?"

I nodded. Bennie nodded. My dad took my arm and guided me to the car. His brown eyes were cold like a judge's. His gripped my arm so hard I felt like a criminal, a slug, a thoroughly mean dude. I gulped twice, shifted the towel. "I should take the frozen peas back to the school. The secretary might need them for some other kid."

Dad didn't say anything. He just stared at me. He drove to the hospital slowly. Just before we went inside he turned to me. "Johnny, you have a big mouth, we've always known that. You have big ears, we've always known that, too. But I thought you had a bigger heart. Bennie can't help how he is. Teasing and taunting others about who they are, what they wear, how they smell, what they eat, how they talk, it just doesn't wash. Not with me. You weren't called into being to fix other people, Johnny. I'm assigning you to take a good look at yourself. And not just the outside. We'll let the doctor fix that. You sure are a mess." He sounded more like a bank manager than my usual cheerful dad. Tears gathered in my eyes and it wasn't from the pain.

As we walked into the hospital he put his arm around my shoulder. He's like that. He doesn't stay mad at a guy. He had said what he had to say. I heard him loud and clear. Even though my nose, jaw and lips throbbed with pain, it was nothing compared to how I felt inside.

The hospital was fascinating with weird and wonderful people in the waiting room. The place was filled with strong smells of old coffee, damp coats, and disinfectant in the emergency room. The doctor wore a green outfit just like a hospital television show I like. Her stethoscope dangled from a baggy pocket, her tiny earrings sparkled. Dr. Jane asked lots of questions and poked and prodded me. It took hours.

That's how I ended up bandaged like a mummy, wearing this funny head gear, waiting for the plastic surgeon to unwrap my head. She's going to unveil my face the Thursday afternoon after school before the concert. So I can still go to the big event, even if it's too late for me to sing. My dad thought he wouldn't have to go but I want to fix things if I can.

Besides, I want the kids to see my new face before the holidays. I can hardly wait for their reaction. See, the doctor, my dad and I had a little conversation before I went under the anaesthetic and she operated. I haven't even told David Lee what I had done while I was asleep on that operating table, and he's my best friend.

Chapter 2

It was Thursday morning when Bennie hit me. I spent the weekend in the hospital lying flat on my back. The first couple of days they fed me through a tube. I asked if they had chocolate-flavoured intravenous. I should say I whispered. Talking was out of the question. My jaw wasn't broken but it was bruised and my voice sounded like a cross between a magpie and a gerbil. My whole body felt like it had been trashed.

"Normally we'd have you out of here in a day, but you have a low grade fever," Doctor Jane said.

"Better to be safe than sorry," my dad sighed, and brought me Archie comics.

David Lee and his parents came to see me and brought me lemon candies to suck. Doctor Jane wouldn't let me have them until I got unplugged from the intravenous.

Miss Moore and her boyfriend Arthur came too. He's at the Royal Military College, just outside of town. It's where big kids go after high school if they want to be officers in the Canadian Armed Forces. They have high standards, Arthur says. Not just anyone can get in, the competition is tough. Last year's Cadet Wing Commander was a girl who graduated from our school. Mr. Anderson keeps bragging about her.

Arthur sure looked snappy in his blue uniform. His uniform has shiny silver buttons and he wears black boots so polished you can see your reflection in them. I wondered if they took short cadets.

When he and Miss Moore came in my dad was reading *The Hobbit*. It's our favourite book. We read it every year. Now I'm old enough to take my turn reading a chapter.

We were just starting again and Bilbo Baggins was being tempted by Gandalf, the wizard, to go on a journey.

"Have you read the other Tolkien books yet?" Arthur asked. He was standing behind Miss Moore, his big hand on her shoulder. I looked at my teacher. She looked different on a Sunday afternoon, wearing jeans and sweatshirt, her hair windblown, her bootlaces untied. She wore drooping earrings made of seashells. She was blushing, glancing up at her boyfriend like he was a rock star. I guess she's in love. Yuck!

Miss Moore handed me a crazy card about being sick in hospital. Arthur fished in his pocket and brought out a battered copy of *Lord of the Rings*.

"Here, this will keep you out of trouble until you get up and doing."

12

I grabbed it from him. It was tattered and some of the page corners were missing.

"That's terrific," Dad said. "I was planning on starting the *Lord of the Rings* this winter now that Johnny's older." He cracked his knuckles. My dad is a great guy, kind of shy, short and tweedy like a professor but he's really a bank manager. Mom left us the last time he moved from one branch to another. Later she married a widower she met in a French cooking class. They run a restaurant so I eat great when I go there in the summers. I miss her but the last year she was with us it was like she had already left us in her head. I wanted to fix things but I couldn't.

"Johnny, you could come with me," Mom had said.

"I know. But I like the choir, my school, and my friends. Besides you'll have lots of company." Dad had been moping around the house like a spaniel, watching her pack. He needed me. I didn't like her new boyfriend's aftershave or his salt and pepper beard. I went to the wedding but I refused to be an usher.

Too bad Miss Moore has Arthur. She would have been a good match for my dad. I wouldn't mind having her around the house all the time—even if she is young and kind of nervous. She's pretty enough, good at music and knows how to laugh. All the other teachers at Turner are real old, in their thirties at least.

"Who's going to sing Johnny's part?" Dad asked. "He's really sorry about missing that. And he's sorry about teasing Bennie." He glared at me once more. I nodded. I'd gotten the point. I had acted like a jerk.

"It isn't all his fault, Mr. Graham. Bennie hit him. The boy's got a problem with temper. It's not the first time he's blown up. I hate to separate him from the rest of the kids all the time." Miss Moore warmed to her subject. "Miss Dennis says that some classes are easier to teach than others. By next year I'll know a lot more. Experience, that's what I need. I do love teaching music part-time, though. Kids have such good voices. Music soothes them. Even some of the kids with problems." Her arms were waving in the air like they always do whether she's leading the choir or not.

I guess teachers talk about kids the way bankers talk about money. My dad is always yakking about interest rates, the cost of borrowing money and inflation. Come to think of it, I guess I talk about school most the time.

Miss Moore and my dad went on discussing Turner school, the choir, and the winter concert. I could see Arthur was getting restless so I asked him to help me out of bed. I can go for walks but I have to take my friendly intravenous on a pole. Arthur helped me into my housecoat. It's thick like a fat towel and pale blue.

"Thanks," I whispered in my gerbil squeak.

"I guess you won't be coming to the concert?" Miss Moore asked dad.

"Johnny wants to go. In fact he insists. He's hoping to be out of hospital tomorrow. The doctor's keeping him in because he has a temperature. Better not to risk trouble." Dad straightened the sheets on the bed and the four of us walked down the hall, me pushing my chrome pole ahead of me towards the visiting room.

"Arthur can't come to the concert. He's got an important thermodynamics exam on Friday, December the twenty-first." My teacher's voice sounded like Angela

14

Dunn's does when she can't understand a math problem.

"Two exams." Arthur corrected her. He was so tall beside me, I had to take giant steps to keep up to him.

Something metal clattered by the elevators. I twisted around to see what it was. That is when I got a good look at Miss Moore's face. It looked sad, sadder than Bennie Snell when he'd been following us.

"If you don't know the stuff before Thursday, you'll never know it," my dad said. Dad repeats one liners he learned from his father.

"It never hurts to review." Arthur tugged at his mousy-coloured moustache.

"It's a matter of priorities." Miss Moore's voice sounded as if the icicles hanging from the hospital roof were in her throat. "After all, I left home to come and be near Arthur because he asked me. I miss all my friends and my family. It's not easy starting a new job, living in a strange city." She was talking to my dad but her voice carried down the hall. "You are very attentive to Johnny's needs, Mr. Graham. I admire that."

Miss Moore wasn't looking at my dad when she said this. She was talking too loud. Arthur, however—he seemed to miss the whole conversation. Those two needed to figure out how to say what they mean. Like my mom and dad the last month or so they were together, using me as a telephone for goodness sake. 'Tell your father this', and 'Tell your mother that'. Grownups are strange creatures. You need a degree in psychology to communicate with them. Oh, forget it, I had questions of my own.

"How long do you have to go to RMC before you

graduate? Do you sleep in dormitories or do you have rooms? Do they have a height restriction? Can you get married while you are in college?

Arthur laughed. "Alice said you were quite the talker. Now I understand what she meant. RMC, the Royal Military College of Canada, is a four-year degree granting college. It takes students from across the country. You can study arts or science. Most cadets take engineering—civil,

electrical, mechanical or engineering physics. There are several dormitories around a great parade square. Cadets have single rooms. I'm in Fort Haldiman. There are no height restrictions. You can get married during the last year. Okay?"

"Do you like it?" I asked. "I've seen cadets in big coats and capes and funny hats. Sometimes you wear red jackets. Do you dress up all the time? Do you have to iron your own stuff?"

Arthur shook his head. "It's a good education. I get paid while I go to school and I spend summers with the armed forces. Next summer I might get an overseas assignment. Yes, I really like it. It's hard work. Not for the faint-hearted. And you can't mouth off at officers or senior cadets, Johnny."

"I'm not faint-hearted." I whispered. "And I think I've learned a lesson about my big mouth." My voice was giving out again. It gets scratchy.

Losing my voice has made everything that everyone else says and does seem so much more important. I feel ten years older than I did on Thursday morning. Me and my big mouth. The secret the doctor and I have makes me feel strange, too. Being a short kid with mug handles for ears and a big voice has been who I've been all my life. Even in baby pictures.

I remember being real young. I was in a bed with a high side and hanging green turtles, swinging from the ceiling, a net full of stuffed toys, a shelf full of matchbox trucks. Two adults were talking on the other side of the room. One must have been Grandpa Taylor because I can remember the smell of pipe smoke.

"Do you think we should have them fixed, Dad? Do you think they'll be a problem?"

"Hush, my dear. Little pitchers have big ears. Little pitchers have big ears."

I had lain in bed puzzling over what that meant. Pictures hung on the wall downstairs, and over my mom and dad's bed. But they had no ears, and I'd never seen a short pitcher any of the times I sat eating popcorn watching the baseball game in the big park, propped on my dad's lap, wearing my baseball cap and waving a flag. Years later, maybe in Grade Two, I figured out that there was another kind of pitcher, a jug. The saying still didn't make a lot of sense to me but the big ears sure hit home. I was one kid with big ears. It meant I heard well but they look really stupid sticking out like they do.

I rubbed the side of my head gently. Sometimes when the medication wore off I could feel my ears or my nose hurting or buzzing in a numb sort of way. It was my rib cage that really hurt. The surgeon removed part of a rib, carved the bone and implanted it behind my ears. She had to build up the area around the ears so they'd lie flat.

Doctors are fantastic, the way they can fix human bodies, like mechanics repair cars. Or like Gandalf, the wizard in *The Hobbit*, who helped Bilbo change from an average hobbit into an adventurer. I wanted to be a fixer. I sure couldn't be a singer, not this week anyway. But first, I had to set a few things straight.

I turned to Miss Moore who was sitting beside me on the green vinyl couch in the visitors lounge.

"Bennie hit me because I teased him. I teased him really badly. I told him he stunk. I told him he stunk like a bag of garbage, like a skunk."

"Oh, Johnny." She stared at me, nibbling her bottom lip the same way Augusta Cardinal does when she's writing a story.

"It's true, though, he does." Arthur said. "Someone had to tell him sometime."

"Bennie's poor. His mother has too much to do." Miss Moore's thin fingers were lacing and unlacing nervously.

"Your school isn't in the high rent district. It's got a very diverse population," Arthur said. I think he meant that Turner has a real mix of kids in it. That's for sure, especially my class.

"Hitting Johnny wasn't an appropriate response." My dad rubbed his hands on the knees of his trousers. His brown corduroys were worn there. "I've warned you about your mouth, Johnny."

"I know." I hung my head. "I go too far. I need a bodyguard for my tongue. I've got foot in the mouth disease."

"Okay, okay," Arthur laughed. "Johnny, we get the point."

"Couldn't you just say you're sorry?" Miss Moore tousled my hair.

"That's not Johnny's way," Dad said. "Everything that happens is heavy duty, as they say."

The adults chuckled. What's a kid supposed to do? I wanted to fix things like a doctor or a mechanic. Like a wizard, even. After all, I was responsible for the whole mess. I didn't want Bennie Snell getting into more trouble even if he did hit me. I didn't hate the guy or anything. I shook my head.

Then I remembered what Bennie was doing when he came up to me. He was humming, and his humming hadn't been off tune. So I took the plunge.

"Listen to Bennie, Miss Moore. I think he can sing. I heard him humming," I whispered. "He may have hidden talents."

"Everyone deserves a second chance." My dad pulled out another one-liner. This time I agreed with him.

My ears buzzed as if a thousand bees were trapped inside my head, as I struggled back down the hall, leading the three grownups. Dad helped me transfer the tubes from the bathrobe to the nightshirt. I slid into my hospital bed with its scratchy tight sheets. My knees were red from the detergent they used, but then, I've got tender skin. I itched all over. You should see me if my dad forgets to double rinse my underwear. Whoo-ee!

I wanted out of that hospital so badly I could taste it. I wanted to be back home in my own room, and then, quick as a wink back in Miss Moore's classroom with its green boards, the shiny posters of transportation through the ages, the bread basket full of used pencils and pens, the markers in boxes, the coloured paper, the list of class rules, the alphabet in curly letters stretching across the front and along the side wall.

I didn't want the grownups to see but I wanted to cry, 'Take me with you.'

Arthur shook hands with me before he left.

"It takes a pretty big person to admit he caused a fight." He saluted.

"Thanks for the book," I muttered.

I wanted to say something about maybe he should come to the concert, that it was important to Miss Moore that he be there. After my mom left my dad said, "Remember, Johnny, the most important thing in any relationship, whether it's fathers and sons or moms and dads, is that you be there for each other no matter what. Don't forget that one. You have to be there for each other. Your mother and I forgot that. I got too busy with the bank and the Kiwanis Club. We drifted apart and before we noticed it was too late. *Stand By Me* would make a good motto, not just a good movie title."

I wished I could say that to Arthur but I didn't really know him well enough. I sighed.

"Don't worry, Johnny," Miss Moore bent down and patted my bandages. Her perfume smelled like my stepsister's. My mom's new husband's kids are all older— in university or just starting jobs. That's one big reason why I live with my dad. Their house is a zoo. Besides someone had to stay and keep and eye on dad. I'm a joint custody kid. Winters with dad and vacation with mom. Last summer when I stayed with mom and Hugh, her grey-haired husband, I was the only little kid for miles. So I pretended to be old for my age. I played Scrabble, Balderdash, made nachos and talked about God, politics and whether we could clean up the planet in our lifetime.

"I'm okay," I squawked in my magpie voice.

Dad gave me a hug and left with the others. His new brown loafers squeaked all the way down the corridor. Maybe I'll buy him a fancy shoe cleaning kit for Christmas.

I had a nap before dinner. Doctor Jane came in and said I could be unplugged and have a light meal and suck two lemon candies. She watched as the nurse changed the dressings on my head.

"If you are going back to school you have to promise not to run about, get into another fight, or let these come off."

I nodded furiously. The nurse was taping fresh bandages around my jaw.

"Too bad you won't be able to sing. I hear you're pretty good. The kid lands one good punch, and you're out of commission."

"Kids can be cruel," the nurse tut-tutted. "Do you need another pain killer, Johnny?" I nodded. The stitches and tapes made my face itchy and sore. My rib cage felt like an elephant had kicked me. The nurse's crepe-soled shoes made a funny sucking noise on the tiled floor as she went for the medicine. "Poor boy," she said as she walked away.

What the nurse didn't know and what I wasn't going to tell her was I thought Bennie Snell had just given me the best gift in the world. I would never look the same again and that was all right with me.

Chapter 3

When I got back to school Tuesday afternoon the kids were lining up to go to choir practice. My best buddy David laughed as he stared at my wrapped-up head. "You look like one of those cartoon bad guys on Saturday morning television."

"Who's going to sing instead of Johnny, Miss Moore?" Angela Dunn asked from her third place in line. She was wearing purple slipper socks and purple sweatpants. Her pony tail looked like it had been nibbled by mice.

Augusta Cardinal was trying to wash a pen tattoo off the back of her right hand with wet fingers. "No one sings like Johnny," she said.

David Lee bounced on the balls of his feet. The rubber on the bottom of his hightops squealed. "Maybe Johnny will be all right."

"Johnny looks like a mummy," Tyler said." An Egyptian mummy. Ooooh. Woo-oo, spooky or what."

Bennie bent studying his sneakers, avoiding my eyes. His left sneaker had a loose sole. I got into line behind him. I didn't say anything. I didn't know what to say. I felt like I'd been away from the class for a month. Everyone sounded the same. Everyone looked the same. I was different.

"Maybe Johnny's an alien," one of Tyler's buddies giggled. "From a weird planet of know-it-alls."

Miss Moore glared at him and shook her head. She looked worried.

"Who's going to sing Johnny's part?" Angela Dunn asked again. She's hoping it's going to be her. But she goes flat at the end of lines. It makes my head hurt behind my ears.

"We'll manage, Angela. The choir will do just fine." Miss Moore didn't sound very convinced. Her fingers were lacing and unlacing again.

We headed down the hall, stopping for the best singers from Mrs. Dennis's Grade Fives and Mr. Romel's Five-Six split. We slip-slapped our way toward the music room. Tyler dragged his grubby fingers along the wall under the fixed smiles of the school grads from past years; black-framed soccer teams, softball teams and marching bands. I walked at the back of the line with the non-singers and the slow workers. We carried two sheets of math homework and crayons or a library book in case we finished fast. Bennie Snell's sneaker whammed the floor like a beaver banging its tail on the water to warn intruders. All the kids stayed away from us. Bennie, because he smells bad, and me, well maybe they're afraid that head injuries are catching like measles. Maybe because they know I've been a jerk.

I usually walk up near the front of the line. Short and smart near the front. Bennie whirled on me suddenly.

"Why aren't you in front?" he blurted. "You're still

short. You just can't sing, that's all, Johnny Know-It-All."

I smarted from the old insult. I hadn't heard it much for six days, I'd been hanging out with grownups. I glared at him, shocked. After all, I'm the injured party here. What's he want to get rid of me for?

"Bennie, I'm sorry I called you names. Let's forget it, eh?"

"Sure you are."

"I am. But you've got to stop hitting people. It hurts."

"Teach you a lesson."

"A little extreme, if you ask me."

"What do you mean? I don't get it."

"Debate, discuss, decide. Remember." I sighed. This kid wasn't easy.

"I've never been much of a talker."

"Try it. You'll like it."

Miss Moore hushed us as we tiptoed past the open door of the library where the Six Grade kids sat reading. Bennie's sneaker whacked the floor again. The noise echoed .

"Pick up your feet, Bennie," Miss Moore whispered as she came down the hall toward us. I could hear Bennie humming—lines from the songs we were about to sing. I was close enough to get a whiff of old sweat and watch Miss Moore. She was struggling with her face. It quivered around the nose like a hare's. She could smell him, too.

"Where's your work, Bennie?"

We reached the music room. The little kids had left two ukeleles on the floor. Of course, Tyler picked one up and started serenading us, goofing around on stage like he was Michael Jackson. Miss Moore took the ukelele away. While she was busy I stood beside Bennie thinking about the doctor and me, wondering how I could fix things for Bennie. If he could sing, he could learn other stuff. It wasn't his fault. Maybe his parents hit him so he thought hitting was okay. Maybe nobody at his house washed so he didn't know how he smelled.

All the other kids had clustered on the orangish brown carpeted steps at the end of the room.

"Tell her you want to sing, dummy," I whispered. "Tell her." I hurried to grab a hunk of floor in the corner near the drum set.

"Where's your work, Bennie?" Miss Moore asked again.

"I forgot it, teacher." Bennie turned and stared at me, his pale grey eyes blinking. Then he looked up into Miss Moore's lively face. "I could sing. " A sly glance slid across his face, making him look like Wiley E. Coyote.

I watched the two of them as if they were on some TV sitcom. Bennie's skin was the colour of uncooked pies, and his eyes dull like frozen fish. He probably didn't get enough vitamins or sleep. Maybe having my head bandaged was helping my eyes to see past the obvious. Miss Moore, her hand raised as if to ward off some attacker, drew her face away. Her nose twitched. She could smell him like we could. Gross, like used gym socks. What was she going to do? There was a current running among the three of us. I was praying she would ask him to join the choir. She was debating. And Bennie? What was he hoping?

Miss Moore settled the choir in rows, arranging the high voices, the low voices and the extra high in little groups. Angela stood in my usual spot, grinning at me.

Augusta, Vikash and Tyler searched for their low note. I leaned close to the drum set and tried to concentrate on the multiplication I had to finish, tried not to think about how much I liked singing, tried to ignore the scratchy feeling behind my eyes when the pianist started playing the introduction to my solo piece.

Bennie sat beside me, empty-handed, his head bowed. Miss Moore passed him a blank piece of paper and told him to copy the math questions from my sheet and do them. "Finish the math, Bennie. Then we'll decide what to do."

I grinned at him, passed him the math and turned to watch the kids. My ears itched under their bandages and so did my nose. I rubbed the tingly spots carefully. Bennie worked fast and furious. The kid wanted to sing. I urged him on in my head.

Miss Moore opened the music folder on the metal

stand, creased her book flat and glanced at all the choir members. The volunteer mother played the warm-up exercises. My throat ached to sing.

"*Doh-me-soh-me-doh.* Up the scale and down." Her slim hands moved with the notes like they were stair steps in the air. She signalled finish with the usual sweeping motion. "Using *ah, aie, ee, oh, oo,* go up the scale and down." I could see how hard she stared at the kids, trying to keep all of them in her eyes at the same time. A good director has to know where bad notes or bad timing comes from. How I wished I could sing for her. Something about the way she leaned toward the front row made me sure this choir, this concert we were getting ready for, meant a lot to her.

If I hadn't been such a jerk, I could have made it easier for her. None of the other kids sing as well as I do. Maybe that sounds like I'm arrogant but it's true. Augusta Cardinal said I was arrogant in Grade One. That's when I got my nickname Johnny Know-It-All. It's because I got into an argument with Mrs. Dennis about whether children should be able to vote. I said I thought that children over twelve should have the vote so we could stop pollution and cutting down the rain forest. Augusta accused me of repeating something I had heard grownups say. She said that our country was a better place before jerks like me showed up from Europe. Vikash said it was a better place now that immigrants like his parents from India, and from the whole world had arrived. Mrs. Dennis finally got us to shut up. She said she'd never heard such outspoken little kids in her life. Intelligent but mouthy. That's our class. We're still the same bunch. Except for

Bennie. He arrived at Turner School in September.

Bennie had finished scrawling the math questions on his page. He was singing along with the kids, doodling black bugs on the corner of his paper. His voice was pretty good considering he's had no training.

"Sing louder," I whispered. He frowned at me from under bushy eyebrows. I don't think he liked me much. The feeling was mutual. But I felt responsible for him. He better not hit me again, though.

"Bennie's singing," Angela shouted.

"He's supposed to do his math," David muttered. "Only the kids who get their work done can sing in the choir." David's mad that I'm not standing beside him. We make up crazy words for the songs and giggle when the other sections of the choir are practicing their parts.

"Bennie smells," someone said from the middle of the choir. I didn't see the lips move. It could have been Tyler or Vikash. Miss Moore, frowning like Bennie, was studying all the faces as if looking at them would tell her who had spoken out loud. That's our class, okay.

Bennie bent over his paper, his ears bright red, his hand pressing down on the pencil, making black bugs, a string of ugly black bugs. Maybe he thinks that's what we are. My dad says kids are cruel. So did the nurse in the hospital. Maybe we are. I doubt it. Kids are people—they come in good and bad and in between, just like grownups.

"If you've copied that work, Bennie," Miss Moore's voice sounded lower, older, more like Mrs. Dennis's. "If you're finished you could join us." The room grew still. All I could hear was the slosh of the janitor's mop in the hallway.

Bennie grinned like he'd won a ticket to a hockey game, and he moved quickly to the empty spot in the front row—between Angela and David, where I usually stand.

The pianist glanced at the ceiling as if God was going to help her. The kids shuffled and squirmed, moving their bodies away.

"Let's begin with 'Angels we have heard'." Miss Moore lifted her arms wide. Her silent mouth shaped the word 'ready'.

Like a flock of sparrows on a front lawn the three rows of kids burst into song. The notes, the words flowed out, filling the music room. A space behind my ears hurt, I wanted to join in so badly. And I couldn't.

"Don't drag the 'Gloria', high voices. Echo, you are slow on your entry and a little flat. Think high." The teacher stood on tiptoe to encourage everyone.

I'd finished my math so I sat watching every move people made. It was like watching television or watching the grownup kids around my mom's house. When I went to visit last summer, mom didn't know what to do with me. She and her new husband kept mooning around each other like a couple of teenagers in love. I didn't really fit in. So I tried to act like the big kids. I lived a lot in my head, too. Just like now, sitting here on the sidelines watching the choir and the teacher and Bennie.

The practice went on.

"It's *de-o*, not day-o. Watch your enunciation." Miss Moore's hands danced to the melody like they were caught up in the beauty of the notes, the words, the whole sound. Every once in awhile she'd glance down at us. Most of the nonsingers had finished their worksheets and were listening to the music. I rocked back and forth on my knees in time to the music.

Bennie hadn't taken his eyes off the teacher since he'd climbed up the steps to stand between Angela and David. His mouth was forming the words, picking up the tune from the kids around him, studying Miss Moore's hands so he'd know when to come in, when to stop. I don't remember ever seeing him pay that kind of attention in class. I couldn't hear his voice very well, but then I couldn't hear any bad notes either. So he must be singing on key. I can't stand it when someone goes off key. I'm allergic to it.

They ran over the other pieces and I turned my attention to doodling music notes on my page, thinking about how Bennie had been sitting at the back of the class all those weeks and how I'd been singing in the choir. If he hadn't clobbered me, he might have been sitting there still. If he hadn't clobbered me I'd be singing, not sitting on the sidelines with a big smile on my face. I wouldn't have this neat secret.

"What are you grinning about, Johnny?" David asked as we hurried down the hall, avoiding the yellow 'wet floors' signs, trying to make our sneakers squeal as we walked. "You don't have to stand beside Bennie, that's why, isn't it?"

I wasn't going to tell David my big secret. He could wait with the rest of the kids. "Can't a guy be happy, for Pete's sake? Bennie sings okay."

"Yeah, but..." He tried to broad jump over a crack in the tiles.

"Boys," Miss Moore put a calming hand on David's

arm. He stopped mid-slide and walked quietly.

"You have a good voice, Bennie," she said.

"I listened good, eh, teacher?" His cheeks shone red, like they had clown makeup on. I figured the kid was pleased. I know I was.

Chapter 4

Later that day while the kids were out for recess I was helping the librarian glue pockets in the back of the new books in the work room. That was my job for being such a mouthy brat. But I like working in the library so it wasn't a hardship. She had gone to get a fresh cup of coffee. I was reading a new Martyn Godfrey novel.

"I hope you don't need many more practices, Alice," Mrs. Dennis said. She and Miss Moore must have been getting water at the cooler. It gurgled and glubbed in the pause. I put the book down and sat very still. I love listening in on people's conversations. My dad always chases me away from the telephone. I'd listen to everything if I could get away with it.

"I don't want my good singers getting behind." Mrs. Dennis's voice sounded cranky. But that's normal for her. "Too bad about Johnny Graham. He's got such a good voice—even if he is a funny, but difficult child."

"Oh, Johnny's lots of fun in a classroom," Miss Moore said. I blushed hearing them talking about me like that. What was so funny about me? Probably my big mouth, or more than likely my handlebar ears. Well, we'll see about them, the ears, I mean, not the teachers. There's nothing you can do about teachers.

"Have you any other trained soloists? I don't." Mrs. Dennis's voice was fading. She must have walked away from the water cooler. I was tempted to get out of my chair and follow.

"I'm thinking of using Bennie Snell. He has a good voice. Stays on key."

"One of the Snells—sweetly smelling all the while," Mrs. Dennis spoke from the other side of the staff room. "I thought he was a behaviour problem and had difficulty learning."

"I don't want to give up on him too easily. He has a good voice."

"His mother has her hands full. His father comes and goes. The family has been in and out of our school like jackrabbits in a hole. Every time the father gets into trouble with the law the mother takes them back to Enterprise." I could barely hear what Mrs. Dennis was saying, especially with my ears all bandaged. "You can't count on a Snell."

"This is not 'just a Snell', this is Bennie."

I liked my teacher more that minute than I ever had. Mrs. Dennis may have been a teacher for years and years, centuries even, but I'd rather have Miss Moore. She sees each of us, even me with my big ears and big vocabulary, as unique and unrepeatable. She said that the first day of school. Her hands shook a little when she talked to us, introducing herself. Some of the kids giggled. I didn't. It made me think. I'm still thinking about what she said.

"Each one of you is unique and unrepeatable," she said. "You have gifts and weaknesses. All human beings do. In my class we are going to try to foster the gifts and help with the weaknesses. Okay?" The kids stared at her. Pretty big words to use on a fresh bunch of Grade Fours.

The recess bell rang. I put the lid on the glue.

I heard Miss Moore humming tunes from the concert. She was refilling her glass at the cooler. She always has a big glass of water on her desk. The cooler did its funny gurgle and gulp.

"I wonder if the kid has a white shirt? Should I phone his mother? I better ask Arthur." She moved away. I ducked into the hall from the work room and followed her down the corridor.

If anyone could help Bennie Snell with his weaknesses it was Miss Moore. I was trying to do what I could.

Back in the classroom I sat twirling my pencil in my hand as if it was a baton and I was directing an orchestra. *Ta, da, ta dum.*

"Hey, Johnny," Tyler giggled. He shoved my elbow as he passed my desk, accidentally on purpose knocking my pencil on the floor.

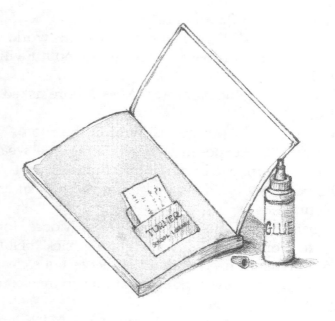

I frowned, the wrinkles in my forehead disappearing into the bandage around my head. The school nurse had replaced the outside bandage with a fresh clean one, to keep down infection, she said. That gave me an idea.

I walked from my desk by the radiator, where I had been sent to consider my sins, over to Bennie's desk by the fish tank.

"Bennie, I sure hope you don't get sick before the concert, now that you are in the choir. I bet you will sing my solo if you keep up the good work."

Bennie looked up from his math problems. His face glowed with sweat from running outside. He smelled bad but I was getting used to it.

"I don't get sick," he said.

"There's a lot of flu around."

"I don't get sick." Bennie hunched over his work.

I coughed once or twice, covering my mouth with both my hands.

"What's the matter, Johnny?" Miss Moore asked. "You sound sick."

"Well, there's lots of germs loose in the room," I said. "And I have been exposed to them. Being in a weakened state I may be prone to bacterial infections."

"Oh, boy," my buddy David mumbled. "What are you up to, Johnny?"

Augusta picked up the theme. "Miss Moore, Johnny's right. We don't want anyone getting sick before the concert. Maybe we need to make sure everyone cleans up, washes hands and covers their mouth when they cough."

"Oh, yuck!" Tyler said.

"We could have a superclean week," I suggested.

"Anyone wearing dirty duds could be fined. Even if we have to wear our white shirts to prove how clean we are."

"White shirts?" Bennie asked. "What white shirts?"

"We always wear white shirts or white blouses with black or blue pants or skirts for school concerts, dummy. Everyone knows that." Augusta said.

"I don't have a white shirt." Bennie said, his voice flat as a pancake.

"I wear my brother's with the sleeves rolled up," said David.

"My mom buys a new one every year." Tyler said.

"Mine makes my shirt." Vikash shouted.

"You can even get them at the second hand store," I said firmly, glancing over my shoulder at Bennie.

"Children, I think we're getting off the track here," Miss Moore interrupted. "We were talking about taking good care of our health for the next week so we can all take part in the concert. What we wear isn't the point."

"I have to take a shower in under two minutes," David said. "My big brother uses all the hot water washing his hair and standing under the shower singing pop songs."

"Every day?" Augusta asked. "Why don't you tell your mom?"

"We could put up a chart," Angela Dunn suggested. "Clean nails, hands, bath or shower, clean undies," she giggled as she said that, " clean socks, shoes."

"Shoes don't count. Who can clean sneakers?" David asked.

"I don't think we should wear our concert clothes." Augusta said. "What if our washer broke down?"

"My mom uses the laundromat on Saturdays." Bennie

sounded like he was talking to himself. Ever since he'd started singing he spent half his time talking or humming to himself. "I guess I could help her. I could take a load there tonight."

My head buzzed. My ears were itchy and my nose scratchy. Maybe I'm growing a moustache under there. This is a great disguise and the kids don't know what is going on. Meanwhile I'm trying to act like Gandalf, the wizard, pushing a little idea here, a little idea there. Is Bennie getting the point? Will he get a white shirt or won't he? Will he sing the solo?

Chapter 5

I was sitting colouring a Santa Claus card for my mom and her bearded husband, Hugh, while the kids were out at lunch time the next day. The room was so quiet I could hear our gerbil chewing seeds in the corner of the room. An empty classroom is quieter than normal quiet. Maybe because it is so full of noise and chatter most of the time. The walls shout.

Our Good Health chart was on the wall. Miss Moore got Disney stickers. It was the first day of the contest so nearly everyone had a row of stickers showing they'd followed all the good health rules. Bennie came in late so he had nothing in his column.

Across the front wall ran the mural we'd made yesterday about festivals—Hanukkah, Christmas,

Ramadan, Chinese New Year, St. Lucia's Day, and Mohammed's birthday. There were recipes for French fudge, Ukrainian bread, Greek baklava and Italian thin crust pizza.

My dad says our country has so many cultures and religions that it is hard to celebrate any of them. I still like Christmas—the story about God loving people so much that the creator sent a nice guy like Jesus to keep them company, and help them. That's pretty good. Santa Claus is a pretty good idea, too. He belongs to everyone, same as Gandalf and Bilbo Baggins.

HEALTH CHART

	MON	TUES	WED	THUR	FRI.		
Augusta		A					
Bernie	A						
Angela							
Johnny							
David							
Tyler			A				
Vikash							
Daniel							

Oh, oh, I was thinking so hard I coloured Santa's boots red instead of black. Johnny, you're a real dip.

"Johnny, what are you doing?" Miss Moore came striding into the classroom, carrying a pile of worksheets. "I thought you were helping the librarian these days."

"She's away. She's ordering computer software for next spring. She's found a whole bunch of CD Roms on science awareness for kids. Stuff about the environment, complicated theories about the extinction of the dinosaurs, fascinating material about the cosmos. I can hardly wait."

Miss Moore chuckled and shook her head. Suddenly I knew what she was thinking. Johnny Know-It-All—the name suits him. I wanted to tell her there was more to me than that. A lot more.

"I'm expecting someone, Johnny." She began erasing the green board in long sweeps.

"Why don't I go read in the library or something?" I said. I'm not totally insensitive. But I wondered what was up. I wondered enough to leave my pack beside my chair.

I paused outside the classroom and scanned the hall. Nobody. Then I heard Miss Moore punching the buttons on the phone on her desk.

"Arthur Shaw, please." There was a pause of a minute or so.

"Arthur, I don't know what to do. I don't know whether to ask Bennie to sing the solo. What if he hasn't got a shirt? What if I embarrass him, or his mother..." There was another long pause.

"I can't ask Mrs. Dennis. She reminds me too much of my mom and you know I can't talk to her. She makes me feel so young and inexperienced. I can't ask anyone. Being the new teacher makes it hard. After Christmas I really have to make the effort—the Grade Three teacher seems really nice. But I've been so busy with the choir, you know. I really want them to do well—so I can prove myself. I wasn't so worried before the fight. If only Johnny hadn't teased Bennie. If only Bennie hadn't punched Johnny. If only I could be sure..." There was another pause while Arthur talked.

"I've got him coming back early. I'm going to have him run through Johnny's solo. See if he can do it." There was another pause.

"No, I don't think I've got things out of proportion. Teaching is my life. This is important to me. I'm really serious about this. It's as important as thermodynamics are to you." I could hear Arthur's voice booming on the other end of the line. I couldn't hear the words, though.

"You just don't understand. You don't understand a thing, Arthur. You don't understand a dog-bone thing."

The receiver banged. I heard her pull a tissue from the box and blow her nose. I hoped she wasn't crying. My mom cried a lot before she left us.

I leaned so close to the door I nearly fell into the classroom. I heard a familiar slap, slap, slap behind me. Bennie Snell came down the corridor. He stopped to slurp at the water fountain. I hurried toward him.

"I need to talk to you."

"Look, Johnny, forget it. I shouldn't have hit you. I know that. You don't have to take care of me. I'm a big kid. I can take care of myself. Maybe hitting you knocked some sense into me. You are a real funny kid. Yappy like a dog. I'll be glad when you get your bandages off. I feel bad every time I look at them. So bug off."

"It's just that I know about singing. I take lessons. I'm in a fancy choir at the cathedral. I want to give you some hints. Don't you want some hints? Don't you want to sing well?"

Bennie sighed, looked hard at me. "Yeah, I do."

"So, can I give you some tips?"

"Okay, okay." He grinned in a kind of lopsided way.

"Bennie, whatever you do, stand up tall when you are singing. It keeps the notes from being pinched in your throat. Relax the inside of your mouth as if you are yawning. Stand with your feet slightly apart and your hands loose at your sides." I hurried away, leaving him standing outside our room staring after me, shaking his head.

I must admit that as soon as I'd finished going to the bathroom I snuck back down the hall and stood outside the door listening to the kid singing. I peeked around the corner of the door. Miss Moore had her keyboard on the table at the back of the room. Bennie stood as close to her as a cat who wants stroking. His eyes shone. He was even trying to stand up tall. It showed in his voice quality. The tone was clearer.

I couldn't help myself, I tiptoed into the room and bent to pick up my backpack from beside my desk. I love music so much, it's harder to stay away from than peanuts. I could feel the inside of my throat tingling with the need to sing. I wanted to join in.

"Johnny," Miss Moore frowned. "I thought you were in

the library."

I lifted my knapsack to show her what I'd come back for.

"Right," she said. "Haven't you heard that curiosity killed the cat?"

"Satisfaction brought it back, Miss Moore." I scrunched my shoulders to show I wasn't really being as lippy as I sounded.

"Johnny, sometimes I think you're really a teenager disguised as a Fourth Grade kid."

"I hang out all summer with my mom's new family and they're all in their teens or in university. They say I'm precious."

"I bet it's precocious." Miss Moore laughed.

"That's right. I'm precocious. That's old for your age, isn't it?"

"That and other things. Someone who is precocious usually knows a lot of stuff. But they are still kids in many ways. Like you, Johnny, like you."

"Is Bennie going to sing the solo, Miss Moore? Is he?" I knew the answer when I looked at the two of them standing side by side. Bennie had a smile as wide as the Rideau River. And so did Miss Moore.

I walked down the hall toward the library, letting my backpack bang against my leg. I hummed the tune from my solo, 'Angels we have heard...', and a discovery, a small discovery came to me, slowly, ever so slowly. I had stood beside Bennie Snell in the corridor. Miss Moore had been standing beside him, close beside him in the classroom.

His face had been clean, his hair had been fluffy and

lighter. There was colour in his cheeks. His grey eyes sparkled. And he didn't smell. He hadn't smelled bad at all.

Chapter 6

The afternoon the kids gathered in the gym for dress rehearsal finally came. I had finished all my homework so I had *Wrinkle in Time* by Madeleine L'Engle in my lap to read while they practised. I wasn't expecting to get much read. I was too interested in watching the choir, watching everyone react to Bennie being the new soloist.

First, the kindergarten kids filled the stage. They tended to wander around, get out of line. One kid sucked her thumb. Two members of the rhythm band dropped their instruments—cymbals and a triangle. The tambourine wouldn't shut up. Two little girls were so shy the teacher had to drag them onto the stage and stick them in the back row. Little kids are so unpredictable.

Not like our bunch. We sat about half way back—comes from being the Grade Four in a school with six grades. We get lost in the shuffle—enough to give us a complex. We aren't tiny and cute or big and responsible. The Grade Six kids spend half their time living their peculiar lives and the other half watching each other to see what's cool and what's not cool. They're like a flock of geese trying to fly in a line so no one will criticise them.

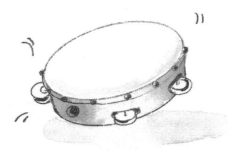

What a bore. I can just imagine what Tyler is going to be like in Grade Six. He'll be a worse tease than he is now. Maybe Dad and I could move.

Finally our turn came. Our class filed past me. David tripped over a chair. Angela's face shone with sweat. The kids walked like some giant puppeteer was pulling them along. I wanted to go, too. My left hand rubbed the bandage under my chin. It still felt scratchy. My ribcage hurt but not as bad as it had. Thank goodness the wrapping comes off soon.

"Go for it, Bennie," I said as he slid past. He grinned so wide I could see his missing tooth.

"Thanks, Johnny," he said, turning back when he reached the aisle. He felt in the pocket of his black sweats and brought out a packet of Smarties. "Here, take these."

I reached out my hand. He dropped the candies into the palm of my hand.

I don't know why but my throat tightened into a knot. The kid had said thanks. The kid with not much money had given me Smarties. Maybe I couldn't sing with the choir, not here and not at the cathedral with all its great

Christmas music. But there was a song bubbling inside, kind of a 'Here Comes Santa Claus' song banging in my ears. Only nobody else could hear it. Just me.

Miss Moore waited by the risers on the stage. Her head nodded as she directed each kid to their place. Mrs. Dennis, the principal and the kindergarten teacher sat together in the front row. I could see the back of their heads. The principal's bald head glistened in the light from the ceiling. The kindergarten teacher's grey hair was pulled back in a tight bun. Mrs. Dennis's hair was fresh blonde from a bottle and sprayed so not one strand could go free. The other teachers were spread around the auditorium keeping an eye on their classes.

The Grade Three teacher, Miss Taylor, filed in with her children. She was unzipping her blue parka. Her kids were excited, their faces rosy from playing outside. She marched them across the front of the auditorium to their reserved chairs. As she passed Miss Moore she leaned over and whispered in her ear, then gave Miss Moore a fast hug, just a little one. Too bad she moved from French Immersion to Grade Three. She might have been a good teacher to have last year. Our teacher went back to university to take graduate studies. Said he needed more child psychology.

My teacher stood, waiting for the kids to finish getting into place. She looked down at the principal and the two teachers in the front row, then out across the noisy gymnasium. Her hands washed each other, her fingers twisting in and out. She shook like she was as nervous as Vikash is each time she asks him to read out loud. Then she glanced at me and grinned.

Miss Moore was one gutsy little lady, I'd say. She'd just started teaching. What a crazy first class to have. And then I let her down by being a mouthy jerk. The least I could have done is sing for her. Instead I was sitting alone in the empty row while all my classmates lined up.

Behind my gauze and tape my face felt hot, my eyes scratchy. Good old Johnny Know-It-All, eh. In some ways I wished the floor would open up and let me drop through. But then again, I had Bennie's Smarties in my pocket.

Miss Moore left the stage and walked to the centre of the front of the room. She turned her back to us. The pianist started the introduction to 'Frosty the Snowman,' our first number. I could see the kids' faces well enough to know what she was telling them. They smiled, they let their hands fall casually , relaxed by their sides. They lifted their shoulders and let them drop loose as a goose. She'd be saying, "Don't pinch the notes or they will go sharp."

They sang. The first verse was a little ragged but that's because they were scared with the whole school and teachers staring at them. My body tensed, holding itself together as if I was singing, too.

The audience clapped. Now, for our big number. First, Mr. Anderson said a few words about honouring all the traditions in the school, not just Christian, ahem, ahem. Then he told the students that Miss Moore and her class would sing two Christmas carols.

Angels we have heard on high
sweetly singing o'er the plains
And the mountains in reply
Echo back their joyous strains.

Bennie and the high-pitched voices came in right on time with

Gloria in Excelsis Deo

Angela and the lower voices echoed—

Gloria in Excelsis Deo

As they finished and the clapping filled the hall Miss Moore turned to look at the audience. Her eyes caught mine. She liked me, even if I had a big mouth and couldn't sing for her. I wished there was something I could do. I watched as she spoke to Bennie. She was probably reminding him to relax his throat, breath from deep down, think of the top of his mouth as a high ceiling filled with air.

She really knows her stuff. Her boyfriend would be proud of her if he could see her now. I am and I'm just in her class.

Bennie stepped forward. The pianist started playing. I held my breath.

The heavenly babe you there shall find
to human view displayed...

Bennie's flute-like notes floated into the gym. His tattered black T-shirt clung to his skinny frame. The loose-soled sneaker tapped the floor in time with the music. His voice wasn't as strong as mine. But let's face it, I've been practising for years.

Mrs. Dennis clapped louder than anyone. Miss Taylor's class shouted 'Bravo!' The whole room filled with clapping as the class filed off the stage and back to their seats. Mrs. Dennis went up and shook Miss Moore's hand. Miss Moore blushed.

"Who would have imagined that Bennie Snell could sing like that," the teacher behind me said under her breath. "Alice has worked a miracle with that class. What a testy bunch they are."

The kids shuffled and squeezed by me. Angela and David giggled. Bennie banged my shoulder with his hand as he passed.

"You were great!" I said. "Nearly as good as me."

"Boy, are you conceited," Tyler waved his fist as if he were going to punch my bandaged jaw. "Someone should teach you a lesson."

"Well, Bennie is good. I said that, didn't I?"

"Never mind, never mind." David handed me a gummy bear. "Shut up, Johnny. You never know when to shut up."

The Third Grade Elves and Fairies trooped on stage in green burlap with jingle bells sewed to their socks. Miss Taylor did a good job of getting them to speak out loud. Our class watched the rest of the show with only our usual amount of whispering, poking and giggles.

"David," I whispered as the Grade Six boys went into their second air guitar number. "We've got to do something for Miss Moore."

David shook his head from side to side. "I'm not getting involved in any of your hare-brained schemes. I always get into trouble with my folks."

"This isn't going to get you into trouble with anyone." I said. "I promise."

He was tying Angela's sneakers to the chair rung. She was sitting in front of us, twirling her hair and leaning over Augusta and two other girls. They were whispering dumb jokes.

Miss Moore was at the other end of the row, keeping Tyler from carving his name on the chair back.

"I just want to ride my bike out to the Military College and visit her boyfriend," I said. "He's a Hobbit fan."

"A hockey fan." David shook his head. "You don't like hockey."

"No, I said a Hobbit, you know, J.R.R. Tolkien."

"I wish you'd talk English for a change," David pulled me up as we followed the line of kids out of the gym. "What's that got to do with helping Miss Moore? Does she need help?"

Angela was trying to untie her shoes from the stupid chair rung. Kids shoved past her. She looked up and shook

her fist at me. I shrugged my shoulders. "It wasn't me." I mouthed.

"I bet," she sneered.

"Angela," Mrs. Dennis went over to her. I hurried from the gym.

Chapter 7

It was home time when we got back to our classroom. So everyone tossed stuff into their cubbies, grabbed coats, took off down the hall. David's mom waited to take him to the dentist.

"I'll phone you," I said. "Maybe I'll come over."

"I'd ask you for supper, Johnny, but we're having Chinese greens and I know you don't like them. Besides David will still be frozen in the face," Mrs. Lee said.

"I'll meet you in the school yard," David said. "Around six-thirty."

I was the last one in the room so I went back and talked to the gerbil. My dad doesn't get home until five and I am supposed to stay next door at the neighbour's until he gets there. She's a nice enough lady but her house is like a furniture store. I perch on the edge of a fancy couch covered with plastic by a lamp covered with cellophane and watch an old television that has no bright colours. So sometimes I dawdle on my way home or visit David Lee. When my mom was there she got home before I did. I miss that. You can't have everything, my dad says.

The gerbil kissed my finger with his funny pink nose, tiny mouth. I sat on one of the chairs close to him and whispered my plans.

"See, I figure if David and I cycle out to the military college we could saunter up and ask to see Arthur, seeing as we were just passing, so to speak." I told the little brown fuzzy animal who was staring at me, his jowls wiggling like a fat dog's. "I could give him back the Tolkien book and ask for another. I haven't finished reading it yet, but he wouldn't need to know that. Then I could tell him that he should come to the concert. That it's important to be there for each other. All he needs is a little nudge, I bet. I'm going to be there at the concert with my dad and we'll clap like crazy. But I guess Miss Moore really wants Arthur there.

"On the one hand, maybe I should mind my own business. But I've never been very good at minding my own business, Mr. Gerbil. On the other hand, maybe if I'd paid more attention to how my mom and dad and I were getting along when I was a little kid, she wouldn't have left. Is that when I started poking my snout into everyone's life? After my mom left?" The gerbil sniffed and sneezed. "Still, I did get Bennie Snell singing. Maybe I'm on a roll."

I heard footsteps in the hall. Mrs. Dennis and Miss Moore entered the room. They stood just by the door, talking. I slouched down in the chair.

"Alice, you take everything too seriously," Mrs. Dennis said. "Your choir is the best Turner has had in years but you still practise too much."

"I want them to feel good about themselves."

"I was as earnest as you are when I started teaching. You are doing an excellent job. Don't worry, the choir will sound great. The parents will love it. The kids will feel good."

"Do you think so? I keep worrying. My mother says I'm a worrywart."

"It is pretty hard to relax the first year. But Mr. Anderson was saying just last night that he hopes you will want to stay at Turner. We did give you that difficult class."

"Oh, I kind of like them. They're unusual."

"You could call them that. Thank goodness the gang you get next year are, what would you call it, an easier mix of kids."

There was a pause. I held my breath. I wanted to tell Miss Moore she was a really great teacher. I felt tears prickling my eyes and I didn't know why.

"I've been wondering whether to offer Bennie extra singing lessons in the new year," Miss Moore said. "Maybe he could come to school early."

"Be careful, Alice," Mrs. Dennis said. "You can't adopt them, you teach them. That's your job."

"I know, I know, but I want to help more. Maybe Turner School should start a clothing exchange, just like the skate exchange. We have several families that rely on the food bank to get through the month. Bennie needs new shoes. Those sneakers are terrible."

"We could talk about that at the next staff meeting. You just concentrate on teaching those children. This class has been a handful since kindergarten. We've each had to take a turn with them. Sometimes a school gets a bunch like this. It isn't one particular child. It's the way they go together. You've got Johnny and David, Angela and Augusta, Tyler the tease. I remember them in Grade One. We wondered whether it was fair to give them to you, seeing as it's your first year. You're doing a good job, though.

"By the way, Angela Dunn told me Johnny Graham tied her sneakers to the chair rung. What will he do next? With Angela blocking the aisle the children couldn't file out in an orderly manner. That boy, sometimes."

"It wasn't me." I stood up at the back of the room. "I didn't do it."

"Johnny, what are you doing here?" Miss Moore jumped in surprise. Mrs. Dennis's face went red.

"Snooping on teachers, young man. What is this class coming to?"

I pulled myself up to my full four feet and marched to the front of the room. I stood beside Miss Moore.

"I was talking to the gerbil at the back of the room. He gets lonely. It's probably bad for him to be left alone so

much. I was keeping him company."

"I'll handle this, Mrs. Dennis, thanks," Miss Moore said.

"Humpf," Mrs. Dennis muttered and left.

"Johnny, you really shouldn't eavesdrop like you do. It's not polite. You hear stuff that you shouldn't."

I nodded my head, shuffled my feet. I couldn't very well tell the teacher that I liked to listen to all that gossip. I forced myself to stare at the floor. I could see three erasers and two pencils on the brown carpet. An old apple lay beside David's sneakers under his desk. I sighed.

Out of the corner of my eye I saw Miss Moore getting ready to either laugh at me or hug me. Her mouth was twitching and her arms were stretched out, palms up half way between a plea and a shrug.

"Johnny Graham, would you please do me a big favour and try to stay out of trouble until after the concert? I need a break."

I nodded my head furiously and dashed out of the room. The room had closed in on me like it was a closet. I hurried away, my footsteps echoing as I headed for the door.

Right after supper I told Dad I was going over to the school to meet David Lee.

"If you're going out I may run back to the bank. The new loans manager needs help understanding our computer system. She's working late."

Under my bandages my ears itched. "Is she young? Is she married?"

"Johnny, mind your own business. I thought kids lived in a world of their own. They are supposed to be more interested in their peers, not in adults. That's what the books say."

"Hey, Dad, that would be like living in a ghetto, wouldn't it? Only kids. Boring. My whole life is lived around adults—parents, stepsisters, teachers, custodians, street crossing guards, bus drivers, storekeepers..."

"Okay, okay," Dad threw up his hands. "Living around us is one thing but trying to run our lives is another."

"Well, doing it on your own you haven't done such a great job, have you?" I took off for my bike before he had a chance to get mad.

When I looked back from the corner he was standing on the front porch. His hands were on his hips and he was shaking his head.

I probably went too far, saying that last bit—it isn't all his fault that he's a single dad. I blew a big bubble with my gum and it burst all over my face. I guess my jaw is working all right. It's my runaway tongue that's giving me trouble.

Chapter 8

David hung from the monkey bars, swinging by his knees. "I thought you'd never get here. I'm supposed to be home by nine o'clock."

We headed over to Princess Street and down to the harbour. It was dark. The Christmas lights on the main street flickered and glowed, red, green, yellow and blue. There wasn't much traffic so we made good time. The smell of seaweed and old fish swept over us as we reached the docks. It was cold as an Arctic midnight. Across the bay the lights of the military college blinked.

"It's going to take ages to get out there." David sounded cranky. "What are we going for, anyway?"

"Trust me and pedal," I said. "Trust me."

Banks of dirty snow from giant snowplows lined the road. The road itself was clear, a little slippery but no snow. The metal grill on the causeway clunka-clunked as our wide tires ran over it. The lift bridge loomed in the darkness. A few stars, a sliver of a moon and hooded streetlights lit our way.

"I might come out here to school when I graduate," I shouted over the wind.

"You're weird, man," David said. "That's ages. You'd have to march on parade and not talk back to grownups. You'd never make it. Besides, kids in Grade Four don't think about stuff like that."

"I do."

The rest of the way out we just pedalled like crazy. My calves felt like jelly by the time we'd reached the edge of the campus.

"Wow, there are lots of buildings. How are we going to find Arthur?"

"The dark ones must be classrooms, gymnasiums, labs. The dorms have lights."

"We're going to get lost."

"Don't be such a pessimist."

We cycled along the walkway by the Memorial Arch and near the seawall. The dark waters of the lake loomed deep and dangerous. The playing fields and Science buildings showed no signs of life. Ahead of us the limestone gatehouse was lit from above by halogen lights. An old guy with a waxed moustache dozed over his notes.

"What now?" asked David.

"We go and ask for Arthur."

"Arthur who?" David asked.

"I don't remember. Starts with an S—Sands or Shaw or Shane. He's Miss Moore's fiancé, that's all I know."

"Will that be enough?"

We leaned our bikes by the wall. Dead vines rustled and cracked. I shivered, pulled my zipper up under my chin to keep out the cold wind off the lake. I spit out my peppermint and knocked on the door.

The old guy's eyes flew open. He jumped like a gun had gone off. He glanced around as if he was expecting someone dangerous—bandits or bullies. I guess he wasn't expecting company.

"We'd like to see Arthur, please," I said in my most pleasing voice.

"Arthur? Arthur who?"

"He's a cadet in his last year and he's a friend of mine."

"Who are you? What do you kids want out here? " The old guy shook himself like a bear waking from hibernation. "This is private property. Belongs to the Department of National Defence. Not for kids."

"I know that." I said, still polite. "I'm a Canadian citizen. My dad pays taxes. I want to see my friend Arthur. His last name starts with an S."

David Lee tugged at my arm, not saying anything. His eyes were huge. "Let's forget it, Johnny."

"I want to return this book." I reached inside my jacket and pulled out Tolkien's *Lord of the Rings*. I checked inside the front cover. Instead of a name it had a number. Maybe it was a secret code.

The old guy's face was getting redder by the minute. "You have no identification. You don't know who you want to see. You drop in here like it was the corner store. What will kids think of next? Go away." He shut the door in our faces. "Come back when you have a name and an invitation, see."

David climbed on his bike and started back down the path. His tires crunched on the gravel. A huge truck lumbering over the causeway made funny noises like thunder, boom-a-boom-a-boom.

I stood outside the gatehouse. I wasn't going to move. I couldn't ride all the way out here, just to turn around and ride back. There had to be a way.

David stopped at the top of the hill and looked back. He shrugged. I heard him groan as he wheeled back down the hill and skidded to a stop beside me.

"Okay, what now?"

I could see the dormitories Arthur had talked about, on either side of the massive square that stretches out toward the point. Fort Frederick is one of several towers along that part of the lake. It stood—lonely, dark and still, jutting out into the lake. A paved road runs behind it. The Martello tower, left over from 1846 when the United States was thinking Canada would make a nice addition to their country, was a great place to picnic. Our family went there when I was little.

"There's more than one way to skin a cat," I hollered and headed down the road to the point.

David cycled after me. "We could get in major trouble here, Johnny."

"Whisper, will you, in case the old dude in the gatehouse comes outside."

A couple of dormitories lay to our right behind the wall. I could see the glare of study lamps, a few heads framed in windows. Maybe this hadn't been such a great idea after all. My legs were tired. I decided we had to take our chances and sneak into the next building.

If we'd had time I would have shown David the boathouses of the college. Sailboats, war canoes, power boats bobbed in the bay or lay upturned on piers. My dad and I had come on a tour when I was in Grade Three.

"Did you know two of Canada's astronauts graduated from this school? Marc Garneau and some other guy..."

"Chris Hatfield. I saw him on television. Johnny, I've got to get home by nine o'clock or I'll be in deep trouble."

"Let's try this one." I hid my bike behind a bush and skipped up the stone steps. I could see cadets bending over desks or lounging in doorways. Some of them looked as tall as giants. At least it was a section with male cadets. I didn't want to bother the girls.

David stood in the shade of a giant oak. "No way. I'm not going in there."

I shrugged and knocked on the first door. "Do you know a guy named Arthur—in his final year?" I added, as the boy with the short haircut and pimples looked up from his open book. He was big as a football player. His polished boots stood like two soldiers by the door. The room was more spotless than I had ever seen a boy's room. Maybe I wouldn't like it at RMC after all. My room was a mess.

"Arthur? Arthur who? What's his number?" He got up and walked into the hallway. A few doors were open. "Do any of you guys know someone named Arthur?"

A blonde guy taller than his doorway chuckled. "How'd this little twerp get in here?"

"Maybe he means Cadet Squadron Leader Art Shaw."

More cadets came to their doors. Down at the end of the hall an old guy in the same kind of uniform as the guard at the gate came striding, swinging some keys, holding a portable walkie talkie. I turned to run back outside. But the cadet with the pimples grabbed the sleeve of my jacket. "Just wait here. This is too interesting to let escape. I was sick of studying anyway."

The tall blonde guy headed up the stairs to the next floor.

"What happened to you, kid?" The cadet who was holding me asked. "Why all the bandages around your head."

"A guy punched me."

"Is this a habit of yours then, sticking your face into places you aren't invited?" The three closest cadets started laughing. They looked like a whole football squad. They clustered around me. I could smell aftershave and bootpolish. My stomach heaved and roared.

"What do you want with Shaw?"

"Come with me, young man." The guard had reached us. He took hold of my arm and started pulling me down the hall. "Where's your friend?"

"Where are you taking the kid, corporal?" my cadet asked.

"They are trespassing on government property. I'm calling the local police and they'll take them back to town." I had wrestled away from the constable and was marching beside him, trying to look older than I felt. What a stupid kid trick. Once again I'd gone too far.

"Wait a minute!" a voice rang out from the second floor landing, a voice I recognised.

"Arthur?" I called. By now the corridor was crowded with cadets. It felt more like a party was happening rather than an arrest. These guys were all buddies and the only idiot was a nine-year-old kid with big ears and a bigger mouth. I wanted to run away. But I started talking fast instead.

"I came to see you," I said as Arthur pushed through the crowd and came to stand beside me. "I brought back your book. I didn't know you'd be so hard to find. I didn't know I was breaking a law."

"Corporal, I can take care of this." Arthur put his arm around me. "I'll bring Johnny to the gatehouse and he can sign in."

"David Lee's outside," I said. "Getting cold."

The cadet with pimples shoved open the door and peered out. "Come in here, kid. It's all right."

David's figure slipped through the door. He looked awfully small surrounded by those tall cadets in their off-duty pants and white T-shirts, short hair, bulging muscles and wide shoulders.

"Didn't know you had little friends in town, Shaw," the tall blonde said. "Thought you spent all your free time with Alice."

"They're in Alice's class at Turner School."

"We're in her choir, too." I said as Arthur led us out the door and along the shovelled path to the gatehouse.

"You just took it in your head to cycle out here and return my book, did you?'" Arthur asked. He assured the two commissionaires that he knew us. We signed in and went back to his dorm to get our bikes. He showed us his room, dug out some chocolate cookies and bought us a can of pop.

I couldn't bring myself to say why I'd come out to see him. The scene with my dad and then with the guards had made me nervous. The college was not designed for mouthy Grade Fours. Besides Arthur was big. He probably wouldn't want some kid telling them him how to run his life. Maybe Dad was right, David was right. I should mind my own business.

Arthur lent me the second book from the Tolkien series. I thanked him "We better be on our way."

"You're sure that's all you wanted?" Arthur asked. He, David and I were walking our bikes back to the gatehouse to sign out.

"How come your book had a number in the front? Is it a secret code?" I asked, ducking the question.

"All cadets have a number. My granddad came here in 1953. His number was 3828. Mine is 18287."

"I might come here. But I'd have to learn how to clean my room."

"They teach you that during recruit training. First at a summer camp before school starts. Some can't stand the discipline and hard work. They leave. The first six weeks of RMC are terrible. Running the square, marching, taking orders, cleaning your boots and your room. They have a team contest at the end."

I nodded.

"I've got to get home, or my life will be terrible, too." David climbed on his bike. "Miss Moore says we sing like angels. See you Thursday night, eh, Arthur?"

"It's important to be there for each other. Miss Moore is a good director." I said as loud as my bandages would let me. I couldn't say anything more.

Arthur glanced back and forth between the two of us. He shook his head, looking real puzzled, then hurried inside.

We cycled like madmen all the way back, parted at the school and I rode home. I poured myself one tall glass of orange juice. Dad sat in the living room reading the paper.

"Where were you?" he asked. "Your face is red like you've been playing hard."

"Just riding around." I said. My dad was quiet, stand-offish. He was still hurting from what I said to him. If it was physically possible to kick myself up the stairs I would have. What a klutz. I can't fix Miss Moore's life. I can't even fix my own. When you only have a dad to live with, you shouldn't make him feel bad.

I went to bed but I didn't go to sleep right away. My ears were itchy and my jaw felt hot. Tomorrow I would get the whole kit and caboodle off and I was sure looking forward to that.

Chapter 9

"Don't forget to wear your white shirt or blouse tonight." Miss Moore circled the room like a caged tiger. The class was more hyperactive than usual. I was glad I was leaving after recess. I would have gotten into trouble if I had stayed. I chewed my lip as I glued pictures of good health habits onto red poster board. I was still sitting in my special place by the radiator. Bennie and I had more in common than ever. Maybe after the holidays we could both manage to sit with the rest of the kids and not get into trouble.

"Cat got your tongue?" Tyler shoved my elbow as he sauntered past. I glued a toothbrush to the top of my desk. My pencil fell on the floor. I jumped up to say something.

"Forget it, Johnny, he's just trying to get your goat," David whispered.

I glared at Tyler and marched to the back of the class and joined Angela and Augusta and a couple of other kids who were making tree decorations.

"I've only got black sweats, Miss Moore," Bennie said, "and a white turtle neck with a tiny alligator on the pocket. Will that be all right?"

I grinned. One of my plans had worked okay. Bennie was pleased with himself, the great soloist. He didn't smell half bad and he talked up a storm. He never used to say much of anything. Maybe we'll trade places—I'll learn to shut up and he'll speak his mind.

Too bad I couldn't really talk to Arthur about the concert. I got out there and I couldn't say anything. Well, as dad would say, you can't have everything.

The bell rang for recess and the kids filed out. "Johnny and David, I want to speak to you?" Miss Moore called.

"Oh, oh," David moaned.

"Yes, Miss Moore?" I stared up into her brown eyes. The lashes curled towards the ceiling. A horse fly slept up there beside the fluorescent light. If I had a stepladder I could get rid of it.

"What's this I hear? You drove out to see Arthur last night?" Her forehead was scrunched up as if she couldn't figure us out.

"Yeah, well, I wanted to take back his book," I said, trying to sound as innocent as possible.

"Nearly got us arrested," David mumbled. "Nearly got us handed over to the police."

"Johnny, what were you up to?" Her eyes flashed. Was

it anger or amusement? I couldn't tell.

"We were inviting him to the concert again," David said. "Johnny said you needed help. I don't know. I just went along for the ride, Miss Moore. My dad says I've got to do more thinking for myself, not follow Johnny's lead all the time. That's what he told me last night when I got home after nine o'clock. I can't watch television for three days because of that trip."

"So, Johnny, I need help do I?"

"No, Miss Moore. I didn't say that," I stumbled over my words. The more I said the deeper hole I seemed to be getting into. "I just don't like people to be unhappy, to miss out on something they want. My dad says we should be there for those we love, I mean those we like..." My ears were itching so badly under the bandages I rubbed right through the gauze. "I have to go, Miss Moore. The doctor is going to take off these dumb bandages. My dad's coming to get me."

I skedaddled through the door, grabbed my boots and hit the playground running.

David caught up with me. "Are you okay?"

"Okay."

"Most of the time your ideas are great." He picked up a piece of ice and heaved it at the telephone pole.

"Sorry about last night."

"Yeah, well don't let it happen again." He punched my arm. I headed to the front to watch for my dad's car.

Halfway there I turned and hollered. "Wait until you see my head unwrapped. Be prepared for a surprise."

"What?" David shouted. "Tell me. I don't like surprises."

"You'll see. The rest of the kids don't know anything about it."

My dad honked the horn.

There are two hospitals downtown. One is old and built of limestone. The other, the one my doctor works in, sprawls beside the university. It has new brick wings and older limestone entrances. My feet made no sound on the polished tile floors. I could smell soup and hot dogs as a woman in a pale green uniform wheeled a cart past me towards the children's wing. Dad and I sat in the Outpatients waiting room. I tried reading a month-old *Time* magazine but it was pretty dull stuff about money and jobs. A teenager was reading the only Archie comic in sight.

I waved my feet back and forth in time to the Musak

piped in through speakers above our heads. I wondered whether having the bandages off would hurt. There was lots of tape and some stitches. Had they melted or do they have to yank them out? Would I look all right?

Dad finished reading *Life* and *Macleans*. "How are you feeling about this, Johnny?" he asked.

I shrugged. I wanted a brass band playing music while I was unwrapped. Here's the new Johnny Graham, an older, wiser model with a whole new set of... finally I can say it out loud...a new set of ears. Suddenly I'm grinning like a cat with cream.

"I can hardly wait until the kids see."

"Kids can be cruel," Dad said. "Your mother and I thought about having them tucked in years ago when you were little, but we figured we'd wait and see. Let you participate in the decision. You sure decided fast. You are one gutsy little kid, Johnny, choosing surgery like that."

"You think so?" I sat up taller. "I got sick of the kids teasing me."

"They'll find some other reason to tease."

I shook my head. I didn't want to believe him.

"Johnny Graham," the nurse called. "The doctor will see you now."

"Hi, Johnny, how are things?" Doctor Jane was smiling. I wondered for a moment if she were married but then I saw her diamond and wide wedding band.

I climbed up on a chrome stool with a black rubber top. I sat on the crinkly paper that covered the black vinyl examining table. A nurse stood beside the doctor. She was holding a silver dish shaped like a quarter moon. A tray with implements of torture and cotton swabs lay on a rolly table beside the doctor. A huge light beamed down on me. My toes curled inside my sneakers. My hands gripped the side of the table.

"Relax, Johnny, this is going to be a piece of cake," Doctor Jane said. She began unwinding the bandage, snipping tape. She gave a little tug here, a sharp pull there. "Bend your head this way, bend it the other." The nurse tossed the gauze into a trash can. She had me stand on a stool while she worked on my side. "Now, for the nose," she continued. I couldn't hold my breath any longer. I let it out. My stomach had knots as big as baseballs. My hands ached from holding still.

"There we are," she said, pulling back and tilting her head to the left side, surveying the results. The nurse handed me a mirror. "Take a look, Johnny."

My dad came over and stood beside me, so close I could smell his cologne and a hint of orange peels from his lunch. "You look great, Johnny. I just hope you've learned your lesson."

"Yeah, I have. I'll hold my tongue the next time." I thought about the arguments that he and mom had had during the last year they were together. Words can hurt. Bennie and I have more in common than I ever realised. Only I use words to hurt with and he uses his fists. Maybe together we could learn to find other ways to solve things. I kind of like the kid now that he's talking and singing and not smelling so bad.

I held the mirror up and turned my head, first to the left and then to the right. I stared at the mirror face on. The ears didn't stick out at all. They were tucked right in beside my head. They were still pretty big but they were flat. No trace of handlebars. My nose looked pale after all its time under wraps. My whole face looked pasty white.

"You should go to a tanning studio," the nurse chuckled.

"Another satisfied customer I'd say." Doctor Jane slipped off her disposable gloves and tossed them in the trash.

I thanked the doctor like a good boy should and hurried my dad out into a light snow fall. "We better get home and have supper fast," I said. "I don't want to be late for the concert."

"I thought we might go to the rib place seeing as you've

had such a hard time eating for the last little while." I'd majored in macaroni and cheese, mashed potatoes and meat loaf for the last while.

Dad drove along the busy streets like a professional rally driver. The rib place right beside his bank is one of our favourite restaurants. We hadn't been there for ages.

A gang of tellers and loans officers was already in there. I knew most of them.

"Hi, Johnny, how's the face?" the assistant manager asked.

"Come and join us," Lou, one of the older tellers called.

A woman who was hanging up her coat turned around. "So, this is Johnny," she said. "I've heard so much about you." She reached out her hand to shake mine. Her fingers were long, her nails coated with polish. She looked more like a model than a banker.

"Miss Benson, this is my son, Johnny. Johnny, this is our new loans officer." Dad blushed. We sat down at the table, Dad beside Miss Benson and me beside my old buddy, Lou, the teller. I ordered the ribs special.

Johnny, I lectured myself. Keep your mind on the concert and the kids. If your dad has a crush on some beautiful woman it is none of your business. My fingers itched. I bit my lip and studied the assistant manager's tie. It had bulls and purple moons, yuck. I will not stick my nose into other people's business. Especially grownups.

I ate my dinner.

"What's up, Johnny?" Lou asked. "I've never seen you this quiet before. Cat got your tongue? By the way—nice ears, kid."

Chapter 10

Darkness cloaked the sky. As we drove up to the school all the classroom lights were on. I could see kids milling about. The kindergarten had so many decorations in the windows I couldn't see in. Streetlights made pools of light. Coloured bulbs outlined the rooftops of the house nearest the school. Three plywood penguins dressed in scarves and hats serenaded from a neighbour's lawn. I felt more excited about this concert than any I actually had sung in before, even the ones when I had competed for top boy soloist.

The kids filed in silently with their parents. The smell of soap, cologne and Christmas boughs filled the air. Tyler was busy pressing his pencil point into his desk top when I walked into our room. I had left dad and his loans officer Nancy Benson in the auditorium. They were going to save me a seat.

"What are you doing here, Johnny?" Angela Dunn said. She had a red bow in her hair. Made her look different, more grown up or something.

Bennie Snell sat wringing his hands nervously. He looked spotless and scrubbed like a bathroom sink. He still was a very pale dude. His hair stuck out with static electricity. The rotten sneakers had a coat of shoe polish on them and they had new laces.

"You've got your bandages off," he said. "Your nose is okay?" He ducked his head and blushed pink. I guess he remembered who had given me the broken proboscis. When the doctor used that word talking about my nose I hung onto it. It's a great word. I love big words. I'm probably a word freak. I stood waiting for someone to notice the other change to my long-covered face. No one said anything.

Miss Moore came in. David Lee followed her.

"Children, before we go, I want to say something." Miss Moore was dressed really neat in a plain navy blue dress. Her shoes were polished, her earrings twinkly, her hair tidy. No chalk dust on her fingers. Just that diamond ring from Arthur. "I want to say this. You are great kids and whatever you do tonight will be great. I promise to relax if you do. Let's go out there and have fun, sing well and show the whole school what a terrific Grade Four sounds like."

We all clapped.

"We couldn't have done it without you, Miss Moore," said Augusta Cardinal. She can always be relied on to say the right thing to grownups. I should take lessons from her.

"I just came to wish you good luck," I said and waved as I walked slowly to the door. The kids still hadn't said anything about my face. "I'm going now."

David came ambling over to where I was standing.

"Nice nose," he said. There was a pause as he stared hard at my head. "Nice ears, Johnny."

I turned and walked out the door. My ears burned. No one but David Lee had noticed my ears. The operation must have been a failure.

"What about the Know-It-All's ears?" Tyler asked. "I don't get it."

As I left, Miss Moore was lining the kids up. She had put Bennie Snell at the head of the row. He was going to be the star performer. I wasn't even going to be noticed.

All the way to the gym I walked with my head down studying the tiles on the floor. What a letdown. What had I wanted? That's the question my mom's big daughters would ask me. They were studying child psychology or something like that. When kids feel bad they don't ask the right questions, they said.

The auditorium was full of sound. Feet shuffled, chairs creaked, parents coughed or talked too loud. I glanced around the room.

That must be Bennie's mom sitting on an aisle seat. She was going to have a baby and had a gummy-looking toddler with her. Her sweater was missing two buttons. She was there to hear Bennie, though.

Dad waved. Nancy waved. I went to join them, sliding past knees and purses. The Lees sat behind us.

"Nice ears, Johnny," Mrs. Lee said. "It's not everyone gets into a fight and ends up with a new set of ears."

"What was the matter with your ears?" Nancy, the loans officer, asked. She looked genuinely interested. She looked a little bit like Miss Moore but older. She dressed classier and had more makeup. She smelled like fancy perfume. I told her about our class. I told her about the fight and the hospital stay. I told her about Bennie. I started to tell her about Miss Moore but the principal came on and hushed the crowd so he could give his speech. I craned my neck, checking who was here and who wasn't. I sighed.

Arthur Shaw was a stupid guy. I should have hollered at him. I should have screamed at him. How dare he desert his woman? I was so mad at him my ears popped.

Someone from the parents' organisation invited everyone for coffee, juice and cookies after the performance.

Programs rustled, mittens dropped. There were more coughs and someone behind us, probably Mrs. Lee, unwrapped lemon drops. Miss Moore stood whispering to her friend Miss Taylor, leaning by the far wall, keeping an eye on the choir in its two rows of chairs near the front.

The curtain rose. After the kindergarteners and the Grade Ones did their stuff, a small group of children did a

Hebrew dance. A little kid with a big voice read a Hanukkah poem. A Grade Six girl gave a short speech with slides on winter festivals around the world.

Mr. Anderson cleared his throat and stepped up to the mike.

"And now, the Turner choir under the capable direction of Miss Alice Moore, the newest member of our Turner School team." The choir stood as a smattering of applause danced across the auditorium. Suddenly from the back by the door there was a loud clap, clap, clapping. I turned around. Arthur Shaw stood huffing and puffing just inside the door. He was wearing his big black military overcoat, holding his fur hat under his arm. His face was red and wet with sweat. He must have run from somewhere to get here on time.

Miss Moore had glanced around to see who was clapping so loud.

"That's my teacher's fiancé," I explained to Nancy who was trying to follow my head as it swivelled back and forth. "He's got a thermodynamics exam tomorrow."

Nancy laughed. For a moment she focused all her attention on me. "Your dad told me you were quite a character. He told me you had quite a vocabulary. He didn't tell me you were so interested in people. Grownups, even."

I blushed, pressed my lips together. I shrugged and turned my eyes toward the stage where my classmates and the singers from Mrs. Dennis's and Mr. Romel's room were standing still.

Bennie leaned towards Miss Moore. His eyes were big as saucers, his lips were moving. He's probably going over

his lines and all the rules of good singing. Relax your muscles, open your throat. Don't strain for the notes. Let your voice soar like a bird. Say each word clearly. Listen to the voices around you. Don't drown them out.

I sat on the edge of my seat, singing under my breath. When it came time for Bennie's solo I went through all the motions with him. As if that would help. The applause at the end was thunderous. I could hear his little sister calling "Bennie, Bennie," from her mother's lap.

While the Elves and Fairies and the other class acts performed, I relaxed and wondered what kind of cookies they'd have at the party. Mrs. Lee makes big almond ones. Angela Dunn's dad makes real Scottish shortbreads. Tyler's big sister makes chocolate brownies. My stomach growled thinking about the feast.

I raced for Arthur as the crowd started to file out or downstairs

"Great book," I said. "The Tolkien, I haven't finished it yet."

"Great ears," Arthur tousled my hair.

"Nobody but David noticed. It didn't work."

"Sure it did."

"No, it didn't."

Dad and Nancy came up behind me.

"Arguing again, Johnny," Dad laughed.

"If it hadn't worked—the operation, that is," Arthur had his hand on my arm. "If it hadn't worked, then they would have said something for sure. Don't you get it, Johnny? They didn't notice your ears. That's the gift of having flat ears. Nobody notices them."

I stood by the back door of the auditorium with my

forehead wrinkled. Gadzooks, he was right. Arthur was right. What I wanted was ears that didn't stick out. I had them. I had ears that didn't stick out. That's why no one said anything.

I grinned with relief.

Miss Moore came through the doors at the back. Her face was flushed. She'd been running through the halls, I bet.

The grownups introduced each other. Nancy, the loans officer, was taller than Miss Moore. Her voice was lower. Her shoes had higher heels and were shinier. Dad had his arm around my shoulder, I wiggled loose so I could head downstairs for the cookies. No sense letting Tyler and his crowd eat them all.

Arthur was handing Alice a single red rose. It looked like they were alone even though Nancy, Dad and I stood with them.

"Your choir sang beautifully," he said. "David Lee said they sang like angels and he was right. He and Johnny Graham cycled all the way out to the college to tell me that. I thought I better show up—a guy doesn't get to hear angels singing every day of the week. Especially when his fiancée is the angel choir director."

"I thought you had a big exam." Miss Moore said. She was holding his arm as if it was a giant teddy bear. She wasn't going to let go.

"Thermodynamics," I said.

"That and military history," he laughed. "Well, after that visit by my two friends, little angels in disguise as it were, I started thinking about what was important to me. I remembered something you said earlier. Something that made me change my mind." Arthur had draped himself against the door frame. He grinned. "You said something about keeping my priorities straight."

"So you came," Miss Moore said.

"If you don't know your thermodynamics by now you never will," Dad took Nancy's arm and mine and headed for the coffee room. "You have to be there for those you love. That's priority number one. Isn't that right, Johnny?"

I nodded.

When I glanced over my shoulder Miss Moore and Arthur were strolling down the hall towards the teacher's cloakroom. They wouldn't get any cookies but I don't think they cared.

"You did really good, Bennie," I said as I grabbed the last chocolate brownie and an almond cookie in one fist. He was standing by the goodie table wolfing down Mrs. Lee's almond cookies.

Bennie nodded his head. He took a cookie to his little sister and came back.

"Does that fancy choir of yours take new kids?" he muttered as he refilled his juice cup. "If you'd come with me, I'd go." He shuffled his feet, acted like he might take off.

"Why not?" I said. "I'm going back after Christmas. You'd have to audition with the choir master. But dad and I could help you get ready."

Angela Dunn was whispering to Augusta Cardinal and David.

"Nice ears, Johnny," she pointed to my head.

"Still look like elephant's ears to me," Tyler joked, prancing up with his grubby face too close to mine. " The difference is that Indian elephants have ears that stay close to their heads. The African elephants ears stick out like handlebars. I read it in an encyclopedia. Now Johnny Know-It-All looks like an Indian elephant."

That Tyler. Some people never change.

Was I mad? Was I sad? No, I felt pretty good. At least the kids had noticed my ears. I forgot about grownups. I had turned over a new leaf. Leave the grownups to lead their own lives and get on with my own. I drank fruit punch, chased David Lee around the lunch room and ate sugar cookies with Santa Claus faces.

"Who's the pretty lady with your dad?" Angela asked as she tagged me by the recycling bin.

"Is she going to be your stepmother?" Augusta tossed her juice carton into the trash.

I glanced over at Dad and Nancy, the loans officer. They were talking to Mr. and Mrs. Lee. Nancy seemed to be having a good time. If she married my dad she'd have to wear shorter heels. I don't want a mother towering over me. On the one hand, I should mind my own business. On the other hand, that's my dad she's dating.

Maybe I should coax dad into having her over for dinner. I could make my perfect nachos. Then I could disappear and go over to David Lee's and leave the two adults alone. I wouldn't meddle...not me. Not Johnny Know-It-All.

ABOUT THE AUTHOR

Mary Woodbury's books for children include *Where in the World is Jenny Parker?* (Groundwood, 1989), *Letting Go* (Scholastic, 1992), *The Invisible Polly McDoodle* (Coteau, 1994) and *Jess and the Runaway Grandpa* (Coteau, coming out in 1997). She has two books for adults: *The Midwife's Tale* (Wood Lake, 1990) and *Fruitbodies* (River, 1996). A former elementary school teacher, she was born and raised in southern Ontario and lived in Newfoundland and Italy before settling in Edmonton, Canada. She lives with her husband Clair and her terrier Rosie, and is busy writing more great books for kids. She has four sons and five granddaughters.

ABOUT THE ILLUSTRATOR

Barbara Hartmann is the illustrator of a number of children's books, including *Purple Hair? I Don't Care!* (Stoddard, 1994) and *The Abaleda Voluntary Firehouse Band* (Treefrog, 1990) (both written by Dianne Young). She grew up in Pennsylvania and now lives in Edmonton, Canada, with her husband Peter Kaszor and son Daniel.